Uncle Wiggily Longears, the old rabbit gentleman.

DOVER

CHILDREN'S THRIFT CLASSICS

Uncle Wiggily Bedtime Stories

HOWARD GARIS

With a new introduction by
Brooks Garis
Uncle Wiggily Classics, Inc.

Illustrated by Thea Kliros

DOVER PUBLICATIONS, INC.
Mineola, New York

DOVER CHILDREN'S THRIFT CLASSICS
EDITOR OF THIS VOLUME: STEVEN PALMÉ

Published in Canada by General Publishing Company, Ltd., 30 Lesmill Road, Don Mills, Toronto, Ontario.

Bibliographical Note

This Dover edition, first published in 1997, is a new selection of eleven stories reprinted from standard sources. The introduction by Brooks Garis and the illustrations by Thea Kliros have been prepared specially for this edition.

Library of Congress Cataloging-in-Publication Data

Garis, Howard Roger, 1873–1962.
    Uncle Wiggily bedtime stories : unabridged / Howard Garis ; illustrated by Thea Kliros.
        p.   cm. — (Dover children's thrift classics)
    Summary: A selection of eleven of the gentleman rabbit's adventures, including "Uncle Wiggily and the Dentist," "Uncle Wiggily's Accident," and "Uncle Wiggily and the Lost Chipmunk."
    ISBN 0-486-29372-6 (pbk.)
    [1. Rabbits—Fiction. 2. Animals—Fiction.] I. Kliros, Thea, ill. II. Title. III. Series.
PZ7.G182Ume   1997
[Fic]—dc20   96-28386
                                                                              CIP
                                                                              AC

Manufactured in the United States of America
Dover Publications, Inc., 31 East 2nd Street, Mineola, N.Y. 11501

Uncle Wiggily and the Newspapers:
The Adventures of Howard R. Garis
by Brooks Garis

In the early days of this century, America's powerful city papers were the heart and soul of communication. America was in love with the high speed of the written word and virtually every household received at least one paper a day.

My grandfather, Howard R. Garis, was a part of this world. He worked as a reporter on the *Evening News* in Newark, New Jersey, but in the evenings, after his day's work as a reporter was completed, he was a writer of adventure stories under various pen names for the famous syndicator of juvenile literature, Edward L. Stratemeyer.

My grandmother, Lilian Garis, was also a writer and the first newspaper woman in New Jersey. She joined Howard in "ghosting" for Stratemeyer, and together with their two grown children—my father Roger, and his sister Cleo—they became a family of four word-crafters who were dubbed "The Writing Garises" in a 1934 article in *Fortune Magazine*. They penned dozens of popular series: all but the last two volumes of the *Tom Swift* classics, most of the *Bobbsey Twins,* all of the *Baseball Joe* series and many others, a total of over 500 titles.

E. M. Scudder, publisher of the *Evening News,* knew the real hand behind *Tom Swift* and asked my grandfather if he would write some children's stories for the paper, possibly about animals, to run, perhaps, four weeks. My grandfather said he would think about it.

Out for a walk one day and wondering what to write, Howard Garis spotted a rabbit with long, wiggily ears, making his home in a hollow stump. That afternoon, Uncle Wiggily was born, and within a few weeks Uncle Wiggily Longears was hopping off the presses and into the homes of thousands, and eventually millions of children everywhere.

There was a new "Uncle Wiggily Bedtime Story" every working day, six stories a week, and each one ended with a humorous little closing that set the mind spinning and told the title of the next story to come. The *Evening News* had become the first paper anywhere to hand-deliver a serialized bedtime story just in time for Moms and Dads to read their youngsters off to sleep.

The stories were soon running in daily papers around the country and beyond. The tales were amusing and adventurous but not frightening, and the characters had delightful names and charming expressions. Children loved them.

The daily syndication of Uncle Wiggily continued for nearly fifty years, and along the way there were hundreds of books, toys, and the still-popular Uncle Wiggily Game. Shortly before my grandfather died in 1962, he asked my mother, also a writer, to carry on the Uncle Wiggily stories—and so they continue today.

Brooks Garis
Uncle Wiggily Classics, Inc.

Contents

Uncle Wiggily
Bedtime Stories

Uncle Wiggily and the Lost Chipmunk

YOU KNOW when Uncle Wiggily Longears, the old rabbit gentleman, started out to look for his fortune, he had to travel many weary miles, and many adventures happened to him. Some of those adventures you may have heard before, but now I am going to tell you about his travels when he hoped to find a lot of money, so he would be rich.

Uncle Wiggily was walking along the road one morning, after he had slept all night in a hollow stump. He didn't have any breakfast either, for there was nothing left in his valise, and of course he couldn't eat his barber-pole crutch. If the crutch had had a hole in it, like in the elephant's trunk, then the old gentleman rabbit could have carried along some sandwiches. But, as it was, he had nothing for breakfast, and he hadn't had much supper either, the night before.

"Oh, how hungry I am!" exclaimed Uncle Wiggily. "If only I had a piece of cherry pie now, or an ice cream cone, or a bit of bread and butter and jam I would be all right."

Well, he just happened to open his valise, and there on the very bottom, among some papers he found a few crumbs of the honey sandwiches a bumble bee had given him. Well, you never can imagine how good those few crumbs tasted to the old gentleman rabbit, which shows you that it is a good thing to be hungry once in a while because even common things taste good.

"Why, these are ants," said the rabbit.

But the crumbs weren't enough for Uncle Wiggily. As he walked along he kept getting hungrier and hungrier and he didn't know how he was going to stand it.

Then, all of a sudden, as he was passing by a hollow stump, he saw a whole lot of little black creatures crawling around it. They were going up and down, and they were very busy.

"Why, these are ants," said the rabbit. "Well, I s'pose they have plenty to eat. I almost wish I was an ant."

"Well! Well!" exclaimed a voice all at once. "If here isn't Uncle Wiggily. Where did you come from?" and there stood a second cousin to the ant for whom Uncle Wiggily had once carried home a pound of beefsteak with mushrooms on it.

"Oh, I am traveling about seeking my fortune," said the rabbit. "But I haven't been very successful. I couldn't even find my breakfast this morning."

"That's too bad!" exclaimed the ant who wore glasses. "We can give you something, however. Come on! everybody, help get breakfast for Uncle Wiggily."

So all the ants came running up, and some of them

He saw something shining under a blackberry bush.

brought pieces of boiled eggs, and others brought oatmeal and others parts of oranges and still others parts of cups of coffee. So take it altogether, with seventeen million, four hundred and seventeen thousand, one hundred and eighty-five ants and a baby ant to wait on him, Uncle Wiggily managed to make out a pretty fair sort of a breakfast.

Well, after the old gentleman rabbit had eaten all the breakfast he could, he thanked the kind ants and said good-by to them. Then he started off again. He hadn't gone on very far through the woods, before, all of a sudden he saw something bright and shining under a blackberry bush.

"Well, I do declare!" cried the old gentleman rabbit. "I think that looks like gold. I hope I'm not fooled this time. I will go up very slowly and carefully. Perhaps I shall find my fortune now."

So up he walked very softly, and he stooped down and picked up the shining thing. And what do you think it was? Why a bright new penny—as shiny as gold.

"Good luck!" cried Uncle Wiggily, "I am beginning to

"Oh, you poor little dear!" cried Uncle Wiggily.

find money. Soon I will be rich, and then I can stop traveling," and he put the penny in his pocket.

Well, no sooner had he done so than he heard some one crying over behind a raspberry bush. Oh, such a sad cry as it was, and the old gentleman rabbit knew right away that some one was in trouble.

"Who is there?" he asked, as he felt in his pocket to see if his penny was safe, for he thought that was the beginning of his fortune.

"Oh, I'm lost!" cried the voice. "I came to the store to buy a chocolate lollypop, and I can't find my way back," and then out from behind the raspberry bush came a tiny, little striped chipmunk with the tears falling down on her little paws.

"Oh, you poor little dear!" cried Uncle Wiggily. "And so you are lost? Well, don't you know what to do? As soon as you are lost you must go to a policeman and ask him to take you home. Policemen always know where everybody lives."

"But there are no policemen here," said the chipmunk, who was something like a squirrel, only smaller.

"That's so," agreed Uncle Wiggily. "Well, pretend that

I am a policeman, and I'll take you home. Where do you live?"

"If I knew," said the chipmunk, "I would go home myself. All that I know is that I live in a hollow stump."

"Hum!" exclaimed Uncle Wiggily. "There are so many hollow stumps here, that I can't tell which one it is. We will go to each one, and when you find the one that is your home, just tell me."

"But that is not the worst," said the chipmunk. "I have lost my bright, new penny that my mamma gave me for a chocolate lollypop. Oh dear. Isn't it terrible."

"Perhaps this is your penny," said the old gentleman rabbit a bit sadly, taking from his pocket the one he had found.

"It is the very one!" cried the lost chipmunk, joyfully. "Oh, how good of you to find it for me."

"Well," thought Uncle Wiggily with a sorrowful sigh as he handed over the penny, "I thought I had found the beginning of my fortune, but I've lost it again. Never mind. I'll try to-morrow."

So he gave the penny to the chipmunk, and she stopped crying right away, and took hold of Uncle Wiggily's paw, and he led her around to all the hollow stumps until she found the right one where she lived.

And he bought her an ice cream cone because he felt sorry for her. And, just as she was eating it, along came a big, black bear and he wanted half of it, but very luckily the July bug flew past just then, and he bit the bear in the eyes, so that the bad bear was glad enough to run home, taking his little stumpy tail with him. Then the chipmunk took Uncle Wiggily back to her home, and he stayed with her papa and mamma all night.

Now, in case the rocking chair on our porch doesn't tip over in the middle of the night, and scare the pussy cat off the railing, I'll tell you next about Uncle Wiggily and the black cricket.

Uncle Wiggily and the Black Cricket

UNCLE WIGGILY, the nice old gentleman rabbit, was feeling quite sad one morning as he hopped along the dusty road. It was a few days after he had helped the lost chipmunk find her way back home, and he had given her the lost penny which he had also picked up.

"Oh, dear me!" exclaimed Uncle Wiggily, as he thought of the penny. "That's generally the way it is in this world. Nothing seems to go right. I naturally thought I had found the beginning of my fortune, even if it was only a penny, and it turned out that the money belonged to somebody else. Oh dear!"

Well, the old rabbit traveler actually felt so badly that he didn't much care whether he found his fortune or not, and that is a very poor way to feel in this world, for one must never give up trying, no matter what happens.

Then Uncle Wiggily looked in his satchel to see if he had anything to eat, but my goodness sakes alive and a ham sandwich! There wasn't a thing in the valise! You see he was thinking so much about the penny that he forgot to put up his lunch.

"Humph! This is a pretty state of affairs!" exclaimed the old rabbit gentleman. "Worse and worse, and some more besides! I do declare! Hum! Suz! Dud!"

Well, he didn't know what to do, so he sat down on a log beside a shady bush and thought it all over. And the more he thought the sadder he became, until he began to believe he was the most miserable rabbit in all the world.

"Oh, dear! Oh, dear!" exclaimed Uncle Wiggily. "I might as well go back home and done with it."

But no sooner had he said this, than Uncle Wiggily heard the jolliest laugh he had ever known. Oh! it was such a rippling, happy joyous laugh that it would almost cure the toothache just to listen to it.

"Ha! Ha! Ho! Ho! He! He!" laughed the voice, and Uncle Wiggily looked up, and he looked down, and then he looked sideways and around a corner, but he could see no one. Still the laugh kept up, more jolly than ever.

"Humph! I wonder who that is?" said the rabbit. "I wish I could laugh like that," and Uncle Wiggily actually smiled the least little bit, and he didn't feel quite so sad.

Then, all at once, there was a voice singing, and this is the song, and if you feel sad when you sing it, just get some one to tickle you, or watch baby's face when he smiles, and you will feel jolly enough to sing this song, even if you have been crying because you stubbed your toe.

> "Ha! Ha! Ho! Ho! I gladly sing,
> I sing about most anything.
> I sing about a pussy cat,
> Who caught a little mousie-rat.
> I sing about a doggie-dog,
> Who saw a turtle on a log.
> I sing about a little boy,
> Who cried because he broke his toy.
> And then he laughed, 'Ha! Ha! He! He!'
> Because he couldn't help it; see?"

"Well, well!" exclaimed Uncle Wiggily, "I wish I knew who that was. Perhaps it is a fairy, and if it is, I'm going

A little black creature hopped out from under a leaf.

to ask her for my fortune. I'm getting tired of not find-
ing it," and when he thought about that he was sad
again.

But a moment later a little black creature hopped out
from under a leaf, and who should it be but a cricket.

"Was that you laughing?" asked the old gentleman
rabbit, as he again looked in his valise to see if he had
any sandwiches there. "Was it you?"

"It was," said the cricket. "I was just going—— Oh,
kindly excuse me, while I laugh again!" the cricket said,
and then he laughed more jolly than before.

"What makes you so good-natured?" asked the rabbit.

"I just can't help it," said the cricket. "Everything is
so lovely. The sun shines, and the birds sing, and the
water in the brooks babble such jolly songs, and well—
Oh, excuse me again if you please, I'm going to laugh
once more," and so he did then and there. He just
laughed and laughed and laughed, that cricket did.

"Well," said Uncle Wiggily, still speaking sadly, "of

course it's nice to be jolly, anybody can be that way when the sun shines, but what about the rain? There! I guess you can't be jolly when it rains."

"Oh! when it rains I laugh because I know it will soon clear off, and then, too, I can think about the days when the sun did shine," said the cricket.

"Well," spoke Uncle Wiggily, "there is something in that, to be sure. And as you are such a jolly chap, will you travel along with me? Perhaps with you I could find my fortune."

"Of course I'll come," said the cricket, and he laughed again, and then he and the old gentleman rabbit hopped on together and Uncle Wiggily kept feeling more and more happy until he had forgotten all about the chipmunk's penny that wasn't his.

Well, in a little while, not so very long, the rabbit and the cricket came to a dark place in the woods. Oh! it was quite dismal, and, just as they passed a big, black stump with a hole in it, all of a sudden out popped the skillery-scalery-tailery alligator.

All of a sudden out popped the alligator.

"Ah, ha!" exclaimed the unpleasant creature. "Now I have you both. I'm going to eat you both, first you, Mr. Cricket, and then you, Uncle Wiggily."

"Oh, please don't," begged the rabbit. "I haven't found my fortune yet."

"No matter," cried the alligator, "here we go!"

He made a grab for the cricket, but the little black insect hopped to one side, and then, all of a sudden he began to laugh. Oh, how hard he laughed.

"Ha! Ha! Ho! Ho! He! He!" My, it was wonderful! At first the alligator didn't know what to make of it. Harder and harder did the black cricket laugh, and then Uncle Wiggily began. He just couldn't help it. Harder and harder laughed the cricket and Uncle Wiggily together, and then, all at once, the alligator began to laugh. He couldn't help it either.

"Ha! Ha! Ho! Ho! He! He!" laughed the 'gator, and great big alligator tears rolled down his scaly cheeks, he laughed so hard. Why, he giggled so that he couldn't even have eaten a mosquito with mustard on.

"Come on, now!" suddenly cried the cricket to Uncle Wiggily. "Now is our chance to get away."

And before the alligator had stopped laughing they both hopped away in the woods together, and so the bad scalery-ailery-tailery creature didn't get either of them.

"My! it's a good thing you made him laugh," said the rabbit when they were safely away.

"It's a good thing to make anybody laugh," said the black cricket, and then he and Uncle Wiggily went on to seek the old gentleman rabbit's fortune.

And in the next story, in case the sunshine doesn't make my pussy cat sneeze and spill his milk on the new door mat, I'll tell you all about Uncle Wiggily and the doll doctor.

Before the alligator had stopped they hopped away.

[*Uncle Wiggily became quite rich, you know, having found his fortune of about a million yellow carrots, so he fixed up the hollow stump a bit and Nurse Jane Fuzzy Wuzzy, the kind old muskrat lady, came to stay with him and kept the hollow stump nice and tidy. Uncle Wiggily could also afford to have an auto.*

And it was the nicest auto you could imagine. It had a turnip for a steering wheel, and whenever Uncle Wiggily got hungry he could take a bite of turnip. Sometimes after a long trip the steering wheel would be all eaten up, and old Circus Dog Percival, who mended broken autos, would have to put on a new wheel.

And to make a noise, so that no one would get run over by his machine, Uncle Wiggily had a cow's horn fastened on his auto; so instead of going "Honk-honk!" like a duck, it went "Moo-moo!" like a bossy cow at suppertime.]

Uncle Wiggily and the Doll Doctor

"**N**ow, I wonder where I will go to-day?" said Uncle Wiggily, the old gentleman rabbit to himself, as he went along, in his automobile, turning around the corner by an old black stump-house, where lived a nice owl school teacher lady. "I wonder where I had better go? I have it! I'll call on Grandfather Goosey Gander and play a game of Scotch checkers!" and off he went.

It was generally that way with Uncle Wiggily. He would start off pretending he had no place in particular to go, but he would generally end up at Grandpa Goosey's house.

There the old rabbit gentleman and the old duck gentleman would sit and play Scotch checkers and eat molasses cookies with cabbage seeds on top, and they would talk of the days when they were young, and could play ball and go skating, and do all of those things.

But this time Uncle Wiggily never got to Grandfather Goosey's house. As he was going along in the woods, all of a sudden he came to a little house that stood under a Christmas tree, and on this house was a sign reading:

DR. MONKEY DOODLE. SICK DOLLS MADE WELL.

"Ha! That is rather strange!" exclaimed Uncle Wiggily. "I never knew there was a doll doctor here. He must have moved in only lately. I must look into this!"

12

Uncle Wiggily bravely knocked on the door.

So the rabbit gentleman went up to the little house, and, as he came nearer he heard some one inside exclaiming:

"Oh, I'll never get through to-day, I know I won't! Oh, the trouble I'm in! Oh, if I only had some one to help me!"

"My! What is that!" cried Uncle Wiggily, stopping short. "Perhaps I am making a mistake. That may be a trap! No, it doesn't look like a trap," he went on, as he peered all about the little house and saw nothing dangerous.

Then the voice cried again:

"Oh, I am in such trouble! Will no one help me?"

Now Uncle Wiggily was always on the lookout to help his animal friends, but he did not know who this one could be.

"Still," said the rabbit gentleman to himself, "he is in trouble. Maybe a mosquito has bitten him. I'm going to see."

So Uncle Wiggily marched bravely up to the little house under the Christmas tree, and knocked on the door.

All about him were dolls—dolls—dolls!

"Come in!" cried a voice. "But if you're a little animal girl, with a sick doll, or one that needs mending, you might as well go away and come back again. I'm head-over-heels in work, and I'll never get through. In fact I can't work at all. Oh, such trouble as I am in!"

"Well, maybe I can help you," said Uncle Wiggily. "At any rate I have no doll that needs mending."

So into the little house he went, and what a queer sight he saw! There was Dr. Monkey Doodle, sitting on the floor of his shop, and scattered all about him were dolls—dolls—dolls!

All sorts of dolls—but not a good, whole, well doll in the lot. Some dolls had lost their wigs, some had swallowed their eyes, others had lost a leg, or both arms, or a foot.

One poor doll had lost all her sawdust, and she was as flat as a pancake. Another had dropped one of her shoe button eyes, and a new eye needed to be sewed in.

One doll had stiff joints, which needed oiling, while another, who used to talk in a little phonograph voice, had caught such a cold that she could not speak or even whisper.

"My, what sort of a place is this?" asked Uncle Wiggily, in surprise.

"It is the doll hospital," said Dr. Monkey Doodle. "Think of it! All these dolls to fix before night, and I can't touch a one of them!"

"Why must all the dolls be fixed to-night?" the rabbit gentleman wanted to know.

"Because they are going to a party," explained Dr. Monkey Doodle. "Susie Littletail the rabbit is giving a party for all the little animal girls, and every one is going to bring her doll. But all the dolls were ill, or else were broken, and the animal children brought them all to me at once, so that I am fairly overwhelmed with work, if you will kindly permit me to say so," remarked the monkey doctor.

"Of course, I'll let you say so," said Uncle Wiggily. "But, if you will kindly pardon me, why don't you get up and work, instead of sitting in the middle of the floor, feeling sorry for yourself?"

"True! Why do I not?" asked the monkey doctor. "Well, to be perfectly plain, I am stuck here so fast that I can't move. One of the dolls, I think it was Cora Ann Multiplicationtable, upset the pot of glue on the floor. I came in hurriedly, and, not seeing the puddle of glue, I slipped in it. I fell down, I sat right in the glue, and now I am stuck so fast that I can't get up.

"So you see that's why I can't work on the broken dolls. I can't move! And oh, what a time there'll be when all those animal girls come for their dolls and find they're not done. Oh, what a time I'll have!"

And the monkey doctor tried to pull himself up from

Uncle Wiggily poured some warm water on the glue.

the glue on the floor, but he could not—he was stuck fast.

"Oh, dear!" he cried.

"Now don't worry!" spoke Uncle Wiggily kindly. "I think I can help you."

"Oh, can you!" cried Dr. Monkey Doodle. "And will you?"

"I certainly will," said Uncle Wiggily, tying his ears in a bowknot so they would not get tangled in the glue.

"But how can you help me?" asked the monkey doctor.

"In the first place," went on the rabbit gentleman, "I will pour some warm water all around you on the glue. That will soften it, and by-and-by you can get up. And while we are waiting for that you shall tell me how to cure the sick dolls and how to mend the broken ones and I'll do the best I can."

"Fine!" cried Dr. Monkey Doodle, feeling happier now.

So Uncle Wiggily poured some warm water on the glue that held the poor monkey fast, taking care not to have the water too hot. Then Uncle Wiggily said:

"Now, we'll begin on the sick dolls. Who's first?"

"Take Sallie Jane Ticklefeather," said the monkey. "She needs some mucilage pills to keep her hair from sticking up so straight. She belongs to a little girl named Rosalind."

So Uncle Wiggily gave Sallie Jane Ticklefeather some mucilage pills. Then he gave another doll some sawdust tea and a third one some shoe-button pudding—this was the doll who only had one eye—and soon she was all cured and had two eyes.

And then such a busy time as Uncle Wiggily had! He hopped about that little hospital, sewing arms and legs and feet on the dolls that had lost theirs. He oiled up all the stiff joints with olive oil, and one doll, whose eyes had fallen back in her head, Uncle Wiggily fixed as nicely as you please. Only by mistake he got in one brown eye and one blue one, but that didn't matter much. In fact, it made the doll all the more stylish.

"Oh, but there are a lot more dolls to fix!" cried the monkey doctor.

"Never mind," said Uncle Wiggily. "You will soon be loose from the glue, and you can help me!"

"Oh, I wish I were loose now!" cried the monkey.

He gave himself a tremendous tug and a pull, Uncle Wiggily helping him, and up he came. Then how he flew about that hospital, fixing the dolls ready for the party.

"Hark!" suddenly called Uncle Wiggily.

"It's the girl animals coming for their dolls," said the monkey. "Oh, work fast! Work fast!"

Outside the doll hospital Susie Littletail, the rabbit girl, and Alice and Lulu Wibblewobble, the duck girls, and all their friends were calling:

"Are our dolls mended? Are they ready for us?"

"Not yet, but soon," answered Uncle Wiggily, and then he and the monkey worked so fast! Dolls that had lost their heads had new ones put on. The doll that had

Then he and the monkey worked so fast!

spilled all her sawdust was filled up again, plump and fat. One boy soldier doll who had lost his gun was given a new one, and a sword also. And the phonograph doll was fixed so that she could sing as well as talk.

"But it is almost time for the party!" cried Susie Littletail.

"Just a minute!" called Uncle Wiggily. "There is one more doll to fix." Then he quickly painted some red cheeks on a poor little pale doll, who had had the measles, and in a moment she was as bright and rosy again as a red apple. Then all the dolls were fixed, and the girl animals took them to a party and had a fine time.

"Hurray for Uncle Wiggily!" cried Susie Littletail, and all the others said the same thing.

"He certainly was kind to me," spoke Dr. Monkey Doodle, as he cleaned the glue up off the floor. And that's all there is to this story, but in the next one, if the goldfish doesn't bite a hole in his globe and let all the molasses run over the tablecloth, I'll tell you about Uncle Wiggily and the dentist.

Uncle Wiggily and the Dentist

ONE MORNING Uncle Wiggily, the old gentleman rabbit, awoke so suddenly that he nearly fell out of bed. He gave a jump, and put one of his paws to his mouth, exclaiming:

"My! Oh, my! What can be the matter? Such a pain! Oh, double wow!" and whenever Uncle Wiggily said double wow, instead of single, you might know something extra-extraordinary had happened, such as that the roof had blown off, or that the cat was having a fit. But it was neither of those things this time. It was a dreadful pain that Uncle Wiggily had.

It was a dreadful pain that Uncle Wiggily had.

"Why, what can be the matter with me?" the rabbit gentleman went on. "Oh, what an ache! Nurse Jane!" he called, as he slipped into his dressing gown and fairly tumbled into his slippers. "Come here, Nurse Jane Fuzzy Wuzzy!" he begged. The kind muskrat lady was staying with the rabbit gentleman for a while once more.

"Why, whatever can have happened?" asked the muskrat. "Has the bed fallen down, or has a mosquito bitten you?"

"Worse and worse!" cried Uncle Wiggily. "I have such a pain in my tooth. I must have caught cold when I was out riding in my automobile yesterday. Oh, double wow!"

Nurse Jane Fuzzy Wuzzy came hurrying upstairs from the kitchen, where she was baking some carrot pancakes for breakfast. She was not a trained nurse any longer, and she did not wear the white cap and the blue and white striped dress. She was just a plain nurse, not a trained one, now.

"Oh, please do something for me!" begged Uncle Wiggily, jumping up and down from the pain so that the tassels on his bathrobe went flippity-flop, like a little girl's braids of hair when she jumps the skipping rope.

"Open your mouth," said Nurse Jane.

Uncle Wiggily did so.

"Why, you have a hole in one of your teeth," went on Miss Fuzzy Wuzzy. "You will have to go to the dentist's and have it filled."

"Filled with what?" asked Uncle Wiggily, as he jumped harder than ever. "Ice cream?"

"Mercy me, no!" answered Nurse Jane. "That would make it ache worse than ever. You see the tooth has a hole in it, and the cold air, and the cold water you drink, touch on the nerve, and that makes it ache."

"Oh, please do something!" begged Uncle Wiggily.

"So I have a toothache; is that it?" asked Uncle Wiggily.

"You have—and a bad one," replied Nurse Jane.

"And I shall have to go to the dentist's?"

"You will. But don't worry. He will stop up the hole and you will be all better."

"Oh, dear! I do seem to have the most lot of trouble!" cried Uncle Wiggily. "Well, if I have to go I have to. I'll start right out and see what happens. But I wonder what he will use to fill up that hole?"

"Oh, cotton, or rubber, or gold or silver!" answered Nurse Jane.

"I think I will take gold," said Uncle Wiggily. "Then, no matter how poor I get, I will always have some gold in my tooth. Yes, I'll choose gold."

So off he went to the dentist's office. The dentist was a nice bear gentleman, kind and good, who had long claws so that he could pull out an aching tooth if he had to. But mostly he filled teeth instead of pulling them out, for it is too bad to have to pull a tooth if you can save it.

"Get into this chair, and we will see what is the trouble," spoke the bear dentist. So Uncle Wiggily sat in the chair, and pretty soon he went up—up just as in an elevator.

"Why—why—what happened?" he asked in surprise, and his tooth didn't ache so much now.

"Oh, I just raised the chair up a bit so I could look into your mouth more easily," replied the kind dentist. "You see, my chair I can make high or low as I wish, by pushing on a what-you-may-call-it. I make it high for little animals and low for big ones, like elephants and the like of that."

"Do elephants ever have toothache?" asked Uncle Wiggily, curious-like.

"Indeed they do!" exclaimed the bear dentist. "Why, I had one in here once and I had to use a bushel of shavings to fill a hole in his large tooth, so he could eat peanuts without getting a spasm."

"My! My!" exclaimed Uncle Wiggily, and his pain was not quite so bad now, for you see he was thinking of something else.

"Well, I'll not have to put much gold in that hole in your tooth," went on the dentist bear. "It is a small one."

"It feels large," said Uncle Wiggily, putting the point of his tongue in it. "It feels as big as a shoe."

"It always does," replied the dentist. So he got ready to fill Uncle Wiggily's tooth. First he used a thing like a buzz saw, only different. That was to brush out the hole, and make it nice and clean, just like when mamma dusts the parlor chairs because company is coming. Then the dentist put some cotton, with some nice smelling stuff on it, in the tooth.

The dentist put some cotton in the tooth.

"Does it hurt much?" he asked Uncle Wiggily.

"Yes, quite a bit. But—I—I—can stand it," and with his paws Uncle Wiggily took tight hold of the arms of the chair.

"It will soon be over," said the bear dentist. All dentists say that—even papa's and mamma's kind.

Then he put some gold in Uncle Wiggily's hollow tooth and pushed it in hard, so that it would not come out. Then he did a lot of other funny things, and squirted some perfumery in the mouth of the rabbit gentleman, and a nice lady bear dentist who was in the next room, came in and helped hold Uncle Wiggily's mouth open, for he was tired of holding it himself.

"There you are—all done!" suddenly exclaimed the good bear dentist. "Now it won't ache you again!"

"I am so glad of that," spoke Uncle Wiggily.

Then the alligator jumped up and down.

Well, he was just paying the dentist bear gentleman some money, when, all of a sudden, the door of the office opened, and in came a great big skillery-scalery alligator on the jump.

"Oh!" cried the alligator. "Such a toothache! Such a toothache! Oh, I must bite on somebody! I guess I'll bite on you!" and he looked at Uncle Wiggily. "No, I guess I'll bite on you," and he looked at the bear gentleman dentist. "No, I'll bite on you!" he cried to the lady bear dentist, and really you could not blame him, for she was very nice.

Then the alligator jumped up and down, and waggled his tail so hard that he knocked over a vase of flowers, and cried out:

"Oh, what a toothache! I guess I'll bite all three of you! I must bite some one. I'll bite all of you!"

"Oh, my!" exclaimed Uncle Wiggily. "This is terrible! What shall I do?"

The alligator made a jump for the rabbit gentleman, but the bear dentist caught the skillery-scalery creature by his flipping-flapping tail, and said:

"Here! You let Uncle Wiggily alone! I know what is the matter with you. That toothache has made you so upset and kerslastrated that you don't know what you are doing. That's all—you are not yourself. But I will fix you!"

"Fix me! What will you do?" cried the alligator, holding a clawy paw to his long jaw.

"I will stop your toothache and then you will be a good alligator instead of a bad one, and not want to bite any one," said the bear dentist, and he did so, and when the alligator's tooth stopped aching, which it soon did, he was as good as pie, and so gentle that he even did not want to bite the end off his ice cream cone.

So that's how Uncle Wiggily went to the dentist's, and I've told you all that happened there, even about the skillery-scalery alligator. And on the page after this, in case the moving picture man doesn't take our kitchen sink away to use for a fountain pen, I'll tell you about Uncle Wiggily and the lazy duck.

Uncle Wiggily and the Lazy Duck

THE DAY after Uncle Wiggily had scared the bad burglar fox with the Jack-o'-lantern [Uncle Wiggily was driving the night before with a Jack-o'-lantern on the front seat when a burglar fox jumped out of the bushes. The fox saw the scary Jack-o'-lantern, thought it was a giant, and ran away], the old rabbit gentleman and Lulu and Alice and Jimmie Wibblewobble, the ducks, went for a little ride in the automobile.

For it was Saturday, you see, and there was no school. So they went along quite a distance over the hills and through the woods and fields, for Uncle Wiggily's auto was a sort of fairy machine and could go almost anywhere.

Pretty soon they came to a little house beside the road, and in the front yard was a nice pump, where you could get a drink of water.

"I am very thirsty," said Uncle Wiggily to Jimmie. "I wonder if we could get a drink here?"

"Oh, yes," said Lulu, as she looked to see if her hair ribbon was on straight; "a duck family lives here, and they will give you all the water you want."

Right after that, before Uncle Wiggily could get out of the auto to pump some water, there came waddling out of the duckhouse a duck boy, about as big as Jimmie.

"How do you do?" said Uncle Wiggily, politely to this duck boy. "May we get a drink of water here?"

"Oh—um—er—oo—I—guess—so," said the duck

boy slowly, and he stretched out his wings and stretched out his legs and then he sat down on a bench in the front yard and nearly went to sleep.

"Why, I wonder what is the matter with him?" asked Uncle Wiggily. "Why does he act so strangely, and speak so slow?"

"I can tell you!" exclaimed Lulu, and she got down out of the auto and picked up a stone. "That duck boy is lazy, that's what's the matter with him. He never even wants to play. Why, at school he hardly ever knows his lessons."

"Oh, you surprise me!" said the old gentleman rabbit. "A lazy duck boy! I never heard of such a thing. Pray what is his name?"

"It's Fizzy-Wizzy," said Jimmie, who also knew the boy.

"Why, what a strange name!" exclaimed the rabbit gentleman. "Why do they call him that?"

"Because he is so fond of fizzy-izzy soda water," said Alice. "Oh, let's go along, Uncle Wiggily."

He stretched out his wings and nearly went to sleep.

"No," said the rabbit gentleman, slowly, "if this is a lazy duck boy he should be cured. Laziness is worse than the measles or whooping cough, I think. And as I am very thirsty I want a drink. Then I will think of some plan to cure this boy duck of being lazy."

So Uncle Wiggily went close up to the boy duck and called out loud, right in his ear, so as to waken him:

"Will you please get me a cup so I may get a drink of water?"

"Hey? What's—that—you—said?" asked the lazy boy duck, slowly, stretching out his wings.

Uncle Wiggily told him over again, but that lazy chap just stretched his legs this time and said:

"Oh—I—am—too—tired—to—get—you—a—cup. You—had—better—go—in—the—house—and—get—it—for—yourself," and then he was going to sleep again.

But, all of a sudden, his mother, who worked very hard at washing and ironing, came to the door and said:

"Oh, dear! If Fizzy-Wizzy hasn't gone to sleep again. Wake up at once, Fizzy, and get me some wood for the fire! Quick."

"Oh—ma—I am—too—tired," said Fizzy-Wizzy. "I—will—do—it—to-morrow—um—ah—er—boo—soo!" and he was asleep once more.

"Oh, I never saw such a lazy boy in all my life!" exclaimed the duck boy's mother, and she was very much ashamed of him. "I don't know what to do."

"Do you want me to make him better?" asked Uncle Wiggily.

"Indeed I do, but I am afraid you can't," she said.

"Yes I can," said Uncle Wiggily. "I'll come back here this evening and I'll cure him. First let me get a drink of water and then I'll think of a way to do it." So the duck lady herself brought out a cup so Uncle Wiggily and

Lulu and Alice and Jimmie could get a drink from the pump, and all the while the lazy chap slept on.

"How are you going to cure him, Uncle Wiggily?" asked Jimmie when they were riding along in the auto once more.

"I will show you," said the old gentleman rabbit. "And you children must help me, for to be lazy is a dreadful thing."

Well, that night, after dark, Uncle Wiggily took a lantern, and some matches and some rubber balls and some beans and something else done up in a package, and he put all these things in his auto. Then he and the Wibblewobble children got in and they went to the house of the lazy boy duck.

"Is he in?" asked Uncle Wiggily of the boy's mamma.

"Yes," she said in a whisper.

"Well, when I throw a pebble against the kitchen window tell him to come out and see who's here," went on the rabbit gentleman. Then he opened the package and in it were four false faces, one of a fox, one of a wolf, one of a bear and one was of an alligator. And Uncle Wiggily put on the alligator false face, gave the bear one to Jimmie, the fox one to Alice and the wolf one to Lulu.

Then he gave Jimmie a handful of beans and he gave Alice a rubber ball filled with water to squirt and Lulu the same. They knew what to do with them. Then Uncle Wiggily built a fire and made some stones quite warm, not warm enough to burn one, but just warm enough.

These stones he put in front of the lazy duck boy's house and then he threw a pebble against the window.

"Go and see who is there," said the duck boy's mamma to him.

"I—don't—want—to," the lazy chap was just saying, but he suddenly became very curious and thought he would just take a peep out. And no sooner had he

That lazy duck ran faster than ever.

opened the door and stepped on the warm stones than he began to run down the yard, for he was afraid if he stood still he would be burned.

And then, as he ran, up popped Uncle Wiggily from behind the bushes, looking like an alligator with the false face on.

"Oh! Oh!" cried the lazy boy and he ran faster than ever.

Then up jumped Jimmie, looking like a bear with the false face on, and up popped Lulu looking like a wolf and Alice looking like a fox.

"Oh! Oh!" cried the lazy boy, and he ran faster than ever before in his life.

Then Alice and Lulu squirted water at him from their rubber balls.

"Oh! It's raining! It's raining!" cried the boy duck, and he ran faster than before.

Then Jimmie threw the beans at him and they rattled all over.

"Oh! It's snowing and hailing!" cried the lazy boy, and he ran faster than ever. And then Uncle Wiggily threw some hickory nuts at him, and that lazy duck ran still faster than he had ever run in his life before and ran back in the house.

"Oh, mother!" he cried, "I've had a terrible time," and he spoke very fast. "I'll never be lazy again."

"I'm glad of it," she said. "I guess Uncle Wiggily cured you."

And so the old gentleman rabbit had, for the duck boy was always ready to work after that. Then Lulu and Alice and Jimmie went home in the auto and went to bed, and that's where you must go soon.

And if the pussy cat doesn't slip in the molasses, and fall down the cellar steps, I'll tell you next about Uncle Wiggily and Mother Goose.

Uncle Wiggily and Mother Goose

UNCLE WIGGILY Longears, the old gentleman rabbit, sat in his burrow-house reading the morning paper. It was after breakfast, on a nice, sunny May day, and outside the flowers were blossoming and making perfume and honey for the bees as they nodded their heads in the air. I mean the flowers nodded their heads—not the bees. The bees were far too busy to do that.

"Yes," said Uncle Wiggily to himself, "I think I must get one. They are getting very fashionable and stylish. I certainly must get one for myself," and he let the paper slip down to the floor, and he sat there in his easy chair, sort of thinking to himself, and nodding his head every now and then, as he said, over and over again:

"Yes, I must get one. It will do me more good than riding around in my automobile or going to the seashore."

"My gracious me sakes alive and some horseradish apple pie!" exclaimed Nurse Jane Fuzzy Wuzzy, the muskrat lady who kept house for Uncle Wiggily. She was out in the kitchen, doing up the dishes, and she heard what the old rabbit gentleman had said, though he did not think she had.

"I wonder what it is he is going to do now?" Nurse Jane said to herself. "He's been so funny lately—doing those queer new dances—the corn meal flop, the apple dumpling dip and the machoo-choo slide. I hope he isn't going to do anything more foolish. I wonder what it is?"

But Uncle Wiggily didn't tell Nurse Jane—at least just then. He got up, put on his fur coat—oh, listen to me, would you! A fur coat in May! I mean Uncle Wiggily put on his light coat, and without wearing a hat, which he never did in the summer, out he went, leaving Nurse Jane to wonder what it was he was going to do.

Uncle Wiggily went to a store where they sold toy circus balloons, and of the monkey gentleman who kept the store he asked:

"Have you any flying machines?"

"What do you mean—flying machines?" asked the monkey gentleman. "Do you mean birds?"

"Well, birds are flying machines, of course," the rabbit gentleman said. "But I mean a sort of airship that I could go up in as if I were in a balloon, and fly around in the clouds. I am going to get one of those airships for a change."

"Ha!" exclaimed the monkey gentleman. "You certainly are a queer one, Uncle Wiggily, to want to do that. But I am sorry to say I have no airships."

Uncle Wiggily went to a store where they sold balloons.

"Then I will have to make one," said the rabbit. "Please give me some of your balloons."

Uncle Wiggily took some red balloons, two blue ones, a green one, a pink one and one colored skilligimink, which is a very funny color. It was like the Easter egg dye color into which Sammie Littletail, the rabbit boy, once fell, getting all splashed up.

"I don't see how you are going to make an airship out of those toy balloons," said the monkey gentleman.

"I'll show you," spoke Uncle Wiggily. "I next need a clothes basket. I'll leave my balloons here until I get that. You see," the old rabbit gentleman went on, "I want to surprise my housekeeper, Nurse Jane Fuzzy Wuzzy. She doesn't know I'm going to have an airship," and Uncle Wiggily winked both eyes, sort of comical like, and twinkled his nose as if he were going to sneeze.

He went off to get the clothes basket, and when he had it he fastened the toy balloons to it by strings tied to the handles.

"There!" exclaimed Uncle Wiggily. "You see, the toy balloons will lift up the clothes basket and me in it. That will be an airship."

"But will it sail in the air?" asked the monkey gentleman.

"To be sure it will," Uncle Wiggily said. "To make it go forward I am going to put an electric fan in the back of the clothes basket. The fan will whizz around and push the air away, and when the air is pushed out of the way I can shoot ahead, and I'll be sailing. Now you watch me, if you please."

So the rabbit gentleman tied the balloons to the clothes basket, and he made the basket fast to the ground with some clothes-pins, so it wouldn't go up before he was ready for it. Next he got an electric fan, which goes around whizzie-izzie and makes the air cool on a hot day, and the rabbit gentleman fastened this fan on the back of his clothes basket.

"Now I have my airship," Uncle Wiggily said to the monkey gentleman. "I shall go up and sail to my burrow. I think Nurse Jane will be surprised."

Uncle Wiggily started to climb into the basket.

"Wait! Wait!" called the monkey gentleman, who had sold him the toy balloons.

"What is the matter?" asked Uncle Wiggily.

"You had better take some soft sofa cushions in with you," spoke the monkey gentleman. "You—you might fall in your airship, you know," he whispered, sort of bashful like, "and the cushions would be a good thing to fall on."

"I believe you are right," Uncle Wiggily answered. "Thank you! I'll take a few."

So he put some sofa cushions in the clothes basket.

"Now I am ready!" he called. "Please take off the clothes-pins and I will go up. I am going to sail like the airship-birdmen I read of in the newspaper this morning."

The monkey gentleman took the clothes-pins off the ropes that held down Uncle Wiggily's airship and pop-up it went, lifted by the toy balloons—red, green, blue, orange and skilligimink color.

"Now, here I go!" cried the rabbit gentleman, as he started the electric fan. And, surely enough, through the air he sailed, as nicely as you please, right above the tree tops, in his new airship he flew.

"Oh, this is great!" cried Uncle Wiggily. Pretty soon he was right over his house. "I'm always going to travel this way, from now on," he said. "Airships are fine."

And then, all of a sudden, something happened. Mother Goose, who happened to be flying through the air on a broomstick, that day, accidentally dropped a paper of pins she had just bought. They fell down with

Surely enough, through the air he sailed.

their sharp points on Uncle Wiggily's balloons, that were fastened to the clothes-basket. The balloons burst, "Pop! Pop! Poppity! Pop! Pop!" and down fell the clothes-basket airship, Uncle Wiggily and all.

"Oh dear!" cried Mother Goose.

Right down in front of his own door Uncle Wiggily fell and only for the soft cushions he might have been hurt. As it was, his rheumatism was jarred up a little.

"Oh, my!" cried Nurse Jane Fuzzy Wuzzy, rushing out of the house. "What is this? What has happened, Wiggy?"

"Why, this is my new airship," answered the rabbit gentleman, sort of dazed and puzzled like. "I just made it and I came along to surprise you."

"Well, you surprised me all right," said Nurse Jane. "Now, come in the house and I'll rub your back with witch hazel. You must be all bruised! You had better leave airships alone after this."

"I guess I had," said Uncle Wiggily sadly.

But do you s'pose he did? Not a bit of it. He was right at it again next day, and in the story after this, if the rose bush doesn't scratch the eyes out of the potato salad, I'll tell you about Uncle Wiggily's big bounce.

Uncle Wiggily's Big Bounce

ONCE UPON a time, not so many years ago, there lived in the woods an old rabbit gentleman named Uncle Wiggily Longears. His house was in a hollow stump, and he called it a bungalow, to be proper like and stylish, though Uncle Wiggily did not put on too many airs, for he had the rheumatism. And with Uncle Wiggily lived Nurse Jane Fuzzy Wuzzy, a muskrat lady who kept the hollow stump bungalow nice and tidy for him, getting his meals, and dusting the piano.

One day Uncle Wiggily put on his glasses, took his red, white and blue striped rheumatism crutch down off the bird cage, and hopped out on the front porch.

"Where are you going?" asked Nurse Jane.

"Oh! just for a little ride in my airship," answered the bunny uncle. For Mr. Longears had an airship, as I have told you in another story. The airship was made of an old clothes-basket, and toy circus balloons were fastened to it with strings to pull it up in the air. There was an umbrella to keep off the hot sun, and an electric fan in the back of the basket, going around whizzie-izzie to push the airship. Uncle Wiggily steered it by turning a baby-carriage wheel.

"Going out in your airship; eh?" asked the muskrat lady. "Well, don't go too far."

"I won't," promised Uncle Wiggily. "I think a ride will do my rheumatism good. And while I am up in the air I will be looking around for a nice place in the country for us to spend our vacation."

"Oh, are we going to the country this year?" Nurse Jane asked.

"I think so," replied Uncle Wiggily. "It is some time since I have been to the country, and as Spring is almost here it will be nice to watch the flowers blossoming, to see the green leaves coming out on the trees and hear the birdies sing. Yes, we'll go to the country."

But before he and Nurse Jane went there something else happened to Uncle Wiggily, and I am going to tell you all about it.

The bunny uncle was looking at his airship, and wondering if it had eaten enough talcum powder to make it slip over the clouds easily, when, all at once a voice asked:

"Oh, Uncle Wiggily, may I come with you?"

"Come with me where?" the bunny uncle wanted to know.

"Wherever you are going in your airship," was the answer, and Mr. Longears turned to see Sammie Little-

"Oh, Uncle Wiggily, may I come with you?"

tail, the boy rabbit, looking sort of hopeful like and anxious. "Will you take me with you?"

"Why yes, Sammie," the bunny uncle said in his jolly voice. "Hop in and we'll have a little ride. I am going to look for a place in the country where Nurse Jane and I can spend our Summer vacation."

"Oh, I just love the country!" said Sammie.

"So do I," spoke Uncle Wiggily.

He and the bunny boy hopped into the clothes-basket airship, and up and up they went whizzing. Below them was the ground, with the grass just beginning to grow nice and green.

"That looks like the country down there," said Sammie, after a bit. "Look, Uncle Wiggily."

"It is the country," replied the rabbit gentleman, "And see there is a load of hay."

Surely enough, down under the airship was a man sitting on a load of hay which he was driving to market to sell. And then, all of a sudden something went:

"Pop! Pop! Poppity-pop-pop!"

"My goodness me, sakes alive and some peanut pancakes on the multiplication table!" cried Sammie. "What's that?"

"Those are the toy balloons of my airship," answered the rabbit gentleman. "The balloons have burst from the hot sun, and we are falling. Oh dear!"

"Can't you do anything to stop us?" asked Sammie, his nose sort of trembling like a jellyfish.

"Not a thing!" said Uncle Wiggily sadly. "We must fall, Sammie. And I forgot to put in the soft sofa cushions to make an easy spot to land on. Oh dear!"

Sammie looked over the edge of the clothes-basket. Then the boy rabbit cried:

"Oh, Uncle Wiggily, never mind! Don't be afraid!"

"Why not?" asked the bunny uncle. "Why shan't I be afraid?"

Down, down, down fell the airship.

"Because we are going to fall right on that load of hay the farmer is driving along the country road. That will be a soft place for us to fall on."

"So it will!" laughed Uncle Wiggily. "Now we will be all right, Sammie."

Down, down, down fell the airship with Sammie and Uncle Wiggily in it. Down, down, down, and then, all at once, they landed on top of the soft load of hay, and the farmer driving it was so surprised he did not know what to do.

But did Uncle Wiggily stay on top of the load of hay? He did not. No sooner had the airship landed on it than up it bounced with a big bounce, taking Uncle Wiggily and Sammie with it. Once more they were sailing through the air.

"Well!" cried Uncle Wiggily. "This is funny!"

"Where will we land next?" Sammie wanted to know.

"I can't tell," answered Uncle Wiggily, "but we are falling down again."

And they were, but this time there was no soft load of hay under them, for they had bounced away from it.

"Oh, look!" cried Sammie, once more looking over the edge of the clothes-basket. "There is water below us— a lake—and we are going to fall into that."

"Oh, I hope not!" cried Uncle Wiggily. "But still I guess we are, Sammie. No!" exclaimed the bunny uncle a moment later. "We are going to fall on a little island in the middle of the lake. And as the island has some soft fir, or evergreen trees on it we may land in them and not be much more hurt than if we landed on the load of hay."

And that is just what happened. Down went the air-ship, with Sammie and Uncle Wiggily in it, and, a moment later it had fallen right in a bunch of soft fir trees, and neither the bunny uncle nor the rabbit boy was in the least hurt, and the airship was only scratched.

It had fallen right in a bunch of soft fir trees.

"Well, where are we?" asked Sammie, as he stepped out of the clothes-basket, after the fall.

"We are on an island, in the middle of the lake, in the country," Uncle Wiggily said, "and it seems to be a fine, beautiful place. I did not expect to go to the country so soon, though.

"Yes, Sammie," went on Uncle Wiggily, "we are on a country island. You know what an island is, don't you, Sammie?"

"Yes, Uncle Wiggily, an island is land in the middle of a bunch of water, just as if I dropped a popcorn ball in the middle of the dish of cornstarch pudding."

"Exactly," said Uncle Wiggily.

"Only I haven't any popcorn ball," Sammie laughed.

"Perhaps we may find one later," spoke Uncle Wiggily. "Now what do you say to camping here a little while, as long as we are on such a nice island? Shall we camp here?"

"Oh, that would be fun!" cried the rabbit boy. "I am all done school, anyhow—that is all but the last day, and that doesn't count, so I could stay here with you. The only thing is I ought to let my mamma know where I am, or she might worry."

"That is right, Sammie!" said Uncle Wiggily. "We should never make any worries for mammas. They have enough as it is. It was nice of you to think of that. But we can send some word to her, I think, and I'll also send a message to Nurse Jane Fuzzy Wuzzy. Then you and I will camp on this island for a while; that is, if we can find anything to eat. For all I brought with me in the airship is some cherry pie."

"Oh, cherry pie!" cried Sammie. "That's what I love!"

"But we must have something else besides that," went on Uncle Wiggily. "We'll look around. Perhaps we can find some turnips and carrots and lettuce growing here."

And, while they were looking around on the island, all of a sudden along came flying Dickie Chip-Chip, the sparrow boy.

"He can carry our messages for us, Uncle Wiggily!" cried Sammie.

"Of course I will!" exclaimed Dickie, who was very kind and polite. So Uncle Wiggily told the sparrow boy to tell Mrs. Littletail that Sammie was going to stay camping on the island for a time, and also to tell Nurse Jane Fuzzy Wuzzy, the muskrat lady, that the rabbit gentleman would likewise camp out.

"I'll tell them," chirped Dickie, and away he flew over the hills.

"Now, Sammie," said Uncle Wiggily, "we must make a sort of log cabin, or else a leafy tent, where we can stay while we are camping, for the airship will hardly do to live in. I think we can make a tent of some green

They stacked the branches in the shape of a tent.

branches from the trees. Then we will make a campfire and hunt for something to eat."

"Oh, this will be fun!" cried Sammie, clapping his paws.

Soon he and Uncle Wiggily, with their strong, gnawing teeth, had cut off many branches from a pine tree. These they stacked up in the shape of a tent, leaving a little hole down near the ground, where they could go in and out.

"Now to hunt for something to eat!" cried Uncle Wiggily, "and then to make a fire to cook it."

Leaving the airship in a safe place, Sammie and Uncle Wiggily went hopping along over the lake-island in search of food, for they wanted to save the cherry pie for dessert. And, I am glad to say, they found some wild carrots and some tame lettuce growing not far from where they had made the green tent.

"Now, all we'll have to do will be to cook this, and we'll have a fine meal!" cried Uncle Wiggily.

"Oh, camping out is great fun!" exclaimed Sammie, clapping his paws again because he was so glad.

On the way back to the green tent Uncle Wiggily heard a little voice crying:

"Oh, dear! Oh, what a heavy load I have! I shall never be able to get it home. Oh, dear me!"

"Ha! Some one in trouble!" cried the rabbit gentleman. "I must see if I cannot help them." Looking down, he saw a black ant trying to drag along a big loaf of acorn bread, which the ant was taking home for lunch. But the acorn bread was too heavy for the little creature.

"Allow me to help you," said Uncle Wiggily politely.

"Oh, I'll be so much obliged to you, if you will!" cried the black ant. "And perhaps some day I may be able to help you."

"Allow me to help you," said Uncle Wiggily.

So Uncle Wiggily lifted the acorn bread in his strong paws, and put it in the ant's house for her, and she thanked him very much.

"If ever I can help you, I will," she said, as she closed the door.

"Ha! Ha!" laughed Sammie Littletail. "As if a little ant could ever help a big rabbit gentleman."

"Stranger things have happened," said Uncle Wiggily. "And you must not laugh, no matter who offers to help you."

Well, Uncle Wiggily and Sammie reached their green tent, built a fire and cooked the wild carrots and the tame lettuce. Pretty soon it was night and time to go to bed.

"You lie down in the tent on the green boughs, Sammie," said Uncle Wiggily, "and I will sit up and watch and keep the campfire going. For, if the fire dies down we will be cold, and some bad animals might come and bite us. But no animals will come as long as we have a fire going."

So Sammie went to sleep, and Uncle Wiggily sat by the campfire, now and then tossing on more wood to keep it blazing. But, pretty soon, Uncle Wiggily himself fell asleep. The fire went out, and a bad old fox, seeing it die down, crept up closer and closer.

"Ha! Now for a good meal!" cried the fox. "There is no fire, so I am not afraid."

Well, the fox was creeping closer and closer, and he was almost up to Uncle Wiggily, when, all of a sudden, the black ant, who hardly ever slept, saw what was going on. Then that ant crawled right over Uncle Wiggily's nose, and she tickled him as hard as she could, so that the rabbit gentleman awoke, and, when he opened his eyes, the ant cried out:

"Quick, Uncle Wiggily! A fox is after you! Throw some wood on the fire and make it blaze up brightly. That will scare away the fox."

"I will!" cried the rabbit gentleman, and he did.

As soon as the wood was on, the fire blazed up and the fox was afraid, and ran away, snapping his teeth and lashing his tail. But if it had not been for the little black ant, who awakened Uncle Wiggily in time, I don't know what would have happened to the bunny gentleman and Sammie. Which shows you that an ant can do some good in this world, even if it is only to tickle a rabbit.

And in the next story, if the postage stamp doesn't jump out of the letter box and stick itself on the wax doll's nose, I'll tell you about Uncle Wiggily and the pinching bug.

Uncle Wiggily and the Pinching Bug

U NCLE WIGGILY Longears, the rabbit gentleman, and
Sammie Littletail, the rabbit boy, were walking
along in the country woods on Candy Island in the middle of Sugar Lake, where they had been camping for
some time.

"How much longer are we going to stay here?" asked
Sammie, as he stood up on the end of his little stubby
tail and tied his ears in a hard knot, so the prickly briar
bush would not scratch them.

"Well, until we have a few more adventures," replied
Uncle Wiggily, "I am going to write a book, you see, Sammie, when I get back, and I want plenty of stories to put
in it."

"You are going to write a book?" exclaimed Sammie,
surprised like.

"Yes," answered the old gentleman rabbit, "one all
about my travels and adventures. And I need a few
more adventures to put in it. Then we will sail back
home. But it is very nice here; do you not think so?"

"Oh, yes, I like it very much," answered Sammie.

As Uncle Wiggily and Sammie were walking along, the
rabbit boy suddenly gave a cry, and sprang back so
quickly that he almost knocked over Uncle Wiggily.

"What is it? What is the matter?" asked the rabbit
gentleman, when he could catch his breath, which
almost ran away from him when Sammie bumped into

him. "Did you see a snake?" asked the bunny uncle of his nephew.

"No, but there is a big black bug under that stone, and he might bite me," spoke Sammie. "He looks like a pinching bug."

"I am a pinching bug," spoke the little black creature under the stone, "but I would not pinch you, Uncle Wiggily, nor yet you, Sammie. I am in great trouble," and tears came into the bug's eyes.

"Why, what is the matter?" asked Uncle Wiggily, who always liked to help any one in trouble.

"I am caught fast under this stone," went on the black pinching bug. "Try as I have done I cannot get loose, and, unless some one helps me, I may have to stay here forever."

"Oh, no! Never! forever!" cried Uncle Wiggily. "We will help you to get loose. Here, Sammie! You and I will lift up the edge of the stone, and the pinching bug can then pull out his leg."

Then the rabbit gentleman and bunny boy lifted up the stone, and soon the pinching bug was free.

The rabbit and bunny lifted up the stone.

"Thank you, very much!" he buzzed, as he flew away.

"Humph! That's funny," said Sammie, as he brushed the stone dirt off his paws.

"What is?" asked Uncle Wiggily. "What's funny?"

"Why, the pinching bug didn't say he would do you a favor if ever he could," went on Sammie. "All the other animals, or bugs, you ever helped promised to do something for you."

"O, fie, Sammie!" exclaimed Uncle Wiggily. "It is not nice to do a kindness just because you think you will get one back in return. We should help any one, whenever we can, just because it is good to help them, and not because we are to get something back. Never think of what you are going to get. Just think of what you are going to do or give."

"Oh, excuse me?" asked Sammie, politely.

"You are excused," said Uncle Wiggily kindly, and then he hopped along, leaning on his red, white and blue striped barber-pole rheumatism crutch, and Sammie came following after, like Jack and Jill, falling down the hill.

Well, Uncle Wiggily and his rabbit nephew had not gone very far, before, all of a sudden, out from behind a stump jumped a pessimist. A pessimist, you know, is a funny animal who always thinks something bad is going to happen. A pessimist never smiles, and even when he eats an ice cream cone a pessimist imagines it is going to have the indispepsia, or else that the ice cream is sour.

"Ah, ha!" cried the pessimist, as he jumped in front of Sammie and Uncle Wiggily. "Something bad is going to happen!"

"Oh, don't say that!" exclaimed Uncle Wiggily in his most jolly voice. "Try to be happy. Nothing will happen!"

"Oh, yes there will!" the pessimist animal growled. "I know there will. I am going to carry you both away to my den, and keep you there forever, squeezing out sour lemons for me."

"Would it not be nicer to squeeze out sweet oranges?" asked Uncle Wiggily, cheerfully. "They might make you feel better."

"I don't want to feel better!" growled the pessimist. "I want to be unhappy and sad!" and with that he made a grab, and caught Sammie and Uncle Wiggily in his claws.

"See, I told you something bad was going to happen!" he went on.

"Oh, dear!" cried Sammie, very much afraid.

"Hush! Don't cry," said Uncle Wiggily. "I'm sure it will be all right." But it did not seem so, for the pessimist started to drag off the rabbit gentleman and little boy through the woods.

But, all of a sudden, along came flying the pinching bug, who, a little while before, had been caught under the stone.

"Ha!" cried the pinching bug. "My friend Uncle Wiggily is in trouble. I must save him!" And then that pinching bug flew up, and pinched the pessimist so hard on the end of his tail that the pessimist cried:

"Oh, wow! Oh, please don't! Ouch! Stop it! Oh, I'll be good! I'll be good!"

"Then let Uncle Wiggily and Sammie go!" cried the pinching bug.

"I will! Oh, don't nip me any more!" howled the pessimist.

Then the pessimist let go of the rabbit gentleman and of Sammie, and the pinching bug stopped pinching, and the pessimist ran away in the woods and ate a mustard plaster, he was so unhappy.

But, some time later he turned into an optimist, which is a very jolly sort of a creature indeed, always happy and looking for the silver lining of the clouds. Anyhow, the pinching bug did Uncle Wiggily a favor after all, you see, which shows you that you never can tell what will happen in this world.

And on the page after this, if the rubber hose doesn't tie itself up in a knot, and rub molasses all over the postman's umbrella, I'll tell you about Uncle Wiggily and the lemons.

Uncle Wiggily and the Lemons

"WELL, SAMMIE!" exclaimed Uncle Wiggily Longears, the rabbit gentleman, one morning, as he hopped out of the green, leafy tent, where he and the boy bunny were spending a few days on the country island in Sugar Lake. "Well, Sammie, I think you had better go get a pail of water at the spring, and then I will cook breakfast. It is going to be a hot day, and we will not eat too much. We will rest in the shade all we can."

"Oh, dear!" cried Sammie. "I don't like it to be too hot. But perhaps you can make some more cold ice cream, Uncle Wiggily?" asked Sammie, sort of hopeful like.

"Well, I hardly believe we need more ice cream today, since we had some yesterday," spoke the old gentleman rabbit. "Besides, the fish-hawk, who turned the freezer for us, has flown away."

"That's so!" exclaimed Sammie. "Well, what else is good for hot weather besides ice cream?"

"We will talk about it after breakfast," said Uncle Wiggily. "And then, too, we will begin to plan about going back home in my airship. I think perhaps we have been camping on this island long enough. We will look for another one in the country."

Well, the rabbit gentleman and the bunny boy had a fine breakfast, and Uncle Wiggily washed the dishes by letting them soak in the lake. All of a sudden Sammie cried:

"Oh, Uncle Wiggily, some one is coming!"

"My goodness me, sakes alive, and a jug of molasses!" cried the rabbit gentleman. "I hope it isn't the tiddlewink, who tried to take our hot soup and the cold ice cream!"

"No, it is some one coming across the lake in Grandfather Goosey Gander's red-plush steamboat!" went on Sammie. "And it looks like Nurse Jane Fuzzy Wuzzy, the muskrat lady."

"Ha, then she is coming after me, to tell me to come home, I suppose," went on Uncle Wiggily, somewhat sadly. "Our vacation is over, Sammie."

But when Nurse Jane landed from the steamboat of the old gentleman goose, she said:

"Well, Uncle Wiggily, as long as you are going to stay camping, I thought you might as well be more comfortable. I have brought you some good things to eat, and some more clean clothes. And I am going to stay here with you, to look after you and Sammie."

"That will be nice," spoke Uncle Wiggily. "Did you bring any cherry pie? For I used up all we had in the ice cream."

Nurse Jane swept around the door of the tent.

"Cherry pie is one of the things I have brought," replied the muskrat lady. "And, I also brought some lemons."

"Ha! Then that answers Sammie's question!" cried Uncle Wiggily. "I will give him some ice-cold lemonade when the weather gets hot. That will be as good as ice cream for a change."

"Oh, that will be fine!" cried Sammie, clapping his paws. "I just love lemonade! Lots and lots of lemonade."

"Well, after I get this camp set to rights," spoke Nurse Jane Fuzzy Wuzzy, who was a very neat housekeeping muskrat, "we will see about the lemonade."

Then Nurse Jane put some new green boughs in the beds, swept around the door of the leafy tent and unpacked the things she had brought from home in Grandfather Goosey Gander's steamboat. By this time Grandpa Goosey had started back for the duck-pen where he lived, away across the lake. But first he had a piece of cherry pie.

"And now for the lemonade!" cried Uncle Wiggily, as he came back from looking to see if his airship was all right; and it was, I am glad to say.

"Get the ice, Sammie, my boy!" cried the rabbit gentleman, "and we'll have some lemonade. It is getting quite warm."

Soon everything was in readiness for manufacturing the lemonade, as Sammie would have said had he been talking educated like. Manufacturing means making, you know. There was the ice and sugar, the pitcher and glasses—for Nurse Jane had brought all of them with her—and a spoon with which to stir it.

"But where is the lemonade squeezer," asked the old gentleman rabbit, looking around.

"Oh, I forgot all about that!" cried Nurse Jane, sadly like. "How careless of me! Oh, that is too bad!"

"Never mind," spoke Uncle Wiggily, politely. "I dare

"We'll all jump on the board at once."

say I can squeeze the juice out of the lemons in my paws. I'll try."

Well, he did try, but he could not do it. A rabbit's paws are not made for squeezing juice out of lemons, you know.

"Perhaps I can do it," suggested Nurse Jane. But she did no better. Only a few drops of juice came out—not enough to make lemonade.

"I wonder if I could do it?" said Sammie, the boy rabbit. So he tried. But all he could squeeze out was a lemon seed.

"And we can't make lemonade out of a seed!" cried Uncle Wiggily. "We must try some other way. We'll put the lemon under a board, and we'll all jump on the board at once. Perhaps that will squeeze out the juice."

Well, they tried that way, but even with all three of them going teetertotter up and down on a board over a lemon, still not enough juice came out to make lemonade.

"Oh, dear! I don't believe we can do it," cried Uncle Wiggily. "We are not large and strong enough to squeeze out the juice. Oh, dear!"

"Ha! Perhaps I can help you!" suddenly cried a polite voice, and there stood a nice circus elephant. "What is it you wish to squeeze the juice from?" he asked.

"Lemons, for lemonade," replied Sammie, thirsty like.

"Ha! I can easily do that!" cried the elephant. "I am large and strong. Just let me take the lemons. I'll soon have the juice out for you."

And, putting the lemons under his big, heavy foot, he just pressed down the least bit, the elephant did, meanwhile whistling a merry tune through his trunk, and out of a lemon ran a whole lot of juice. Nurse Jane caught it in a tumbler, and poured it in the pitcher, with water and sugar, and there the lemonade was all nicely made.

And, just as they were going to drink it, giving the kind elephant some, of course, up out of the lake once more jumped the bad tiddlewink, crying:

"Lemonade! Give me lemonade! I must have lemonade!"

He was just going to take away the whole pitcher full, when, all at once the elephant suddenly took another lemon, put it on the ground and stepped on it. And the juice and seeds of the lemon flew right in the face and eyes of the tiddlewink, so that the bad creature cried:

"Oh trolley cars!" and away he rushed to wash the sour juice out of his eyes, which were all puckered up. And then Uncle Wiggily, and the rest of them, drank the lemonade, which was very fine indeed, and they were very happy. But the tiddlewink was not, and he did not deserve to be, I think.

And in the next story, if the candlestick doesn't forget to come back when it goes out walking with the umbrella to see the moving picture show, I'll tell you about Uncle Wiggily's accident.

Uncle Wiggily's Accident

"WOULD YOU mind if I asked how you got here, on this country lake island?" inquired Uncle Wiggily Longears, the rabbit gentleman, of the kind elephant. It was the day after the big creature had so nicely made the lemonade by squeezing the lemons with his big foot, and had driven away the bad tiddlewink by squirting lemon juice and seeds into the eyes of the unpleasant creature. "How did you get here?" asked the rabbit gentleman.

"I swam away from the circus," replied the elephant, humming a merry tune through his trunk.

"Swam away from a circus! I never heard of such a thing!" cried Sammie Littletail, the rabbit boy.

"Nor I," said Nurse Jane Fuzzy Wuzzy, the muskrat lady.

They were both stopping with Uncle Wiggily on Candy Island, in Sugar Lake, where Uncle Wiggily and Sammie had landed after an accident to Uncle Wiggily's airship, as I told you a few stories ago. An accident, you know, is something that happens to you, like an adventure, but quite different.

If you happen to get lost in the woods, that's an adventure. But if you get lost, and, at the same time fall down and stub your toe, that's an adventure and an accident. The falling down part is the accident. I just thought I'd tell you, so you would know.

"Well," said the elephant, waving his trunk, "you may never have heard of a chap like me swimming, but I

"I swam away from the circus," said the elephant.

assure you I can do it." And, just to show that he could, the big creature went in the lake and swam about, with only the tip of his trunk sticking out, so he could breathe.

"Yes, you can do it," said Sammie. "But why did you run away from the circus?"

"Perhaps he does not like to talk about that," suggested Uncle Wiggily, most politely.

"Oh, I do not in the least mind, I assure you," said the big creature, carelessly squirting some water through his trunk. "The truth of the matter is that they did not give me enough peanuts, popcorn balls and pink lemonade in the circus, so I ran away."

"And I don't blame you!" cried Uncle Wiggily. "I think I would have run away myself. But I am sorry we have none of these things here."

"It matters not," said the elephant, kindly. "As long as I can squeeze lemons and have a bit of cherry pie now and then I will be all right," and then he came up out of the lake and stretched in the sun to dry.

Sammie, the rabbit boy, hopped on through the woods, to see if any of his animal friends might possibly have come to Candy Island, which it was called because of the many maple sugar trees growing on it. The elephant went to sleep in the sun, Nurse Jane Fuzzy Wuzzy swept and dusted the green leafy bower tent, and Uncle Wiggily was working around his airship, putting on a new coat and hat of paint.

"What are you doing?" asked Nurse Jane, as she saw the old gentleman rabbit blowing some hot air in the red, white and blue toy circus balloons, that made the airship go up. Uncle Wiggily had mended them with chewing gum after they had burst.

"Why, I am getting ready to take a sail," replied the rabbit gentleman. "We have been on this island almost long enough, and soon we will want to go home I think. I am seeing whether or not my airship will take us up when we want to go."

Then he went on with his work, and when Nurse Jane next looked at him she saw him hanging some Chinese paper lanterns around the edge of the Japanese umbrella that formed the top part of the airship of the rabbit gentleman.

"Well, Uncle Wiggily Longears!" cried the muskrat lady. "What in the world are you doing now?"

"Oh, making my airship look pretty," he answered. "I am going to trim it with the lanterns, and, when it gets dark I will light the candles that are in them, and then, if I sail about, the animal folk will think I am a comet, or something like that."

"Well, I never heard of such a thing in all my life!" cried Nurse Jane, as she did her tail up in curl papers in case she should be asked to go to a party.

"Well, if everything goes right, you shall soon see it as well as hear it," said Uncle Wiggily with a laugh.

Soon the old gentleman rabbit had a number of Chinese lanterns hung about his airship, which was still on the ground. He got the paper lanterns from the Chinese laundry at the other end of the island.

"Now we are ready to light up!" cried Uncle Wiggily. "Look, Nurse Jane!"

With that Uncle Wiggily lighted the candles of the lanterns, and in the woods, which were rather dark, they looked very pretty.

"Oh, how lovely!" cried Sammie, coming back from his walk just then. And a moment later Uncle Wiggily had his accident. A puff of wind waved the lanterns, they tipped over, and the paper sides came up against the lighted candles.

All of a sudden they caught fire, and the whole airship was ablaze in an instant.

"Oh, dear!" cried Nurse Jane.

"Call out the water-bug fire department!" yelled Sammie.

"Help! Help!" shouted Uncle Wiggily. "Oh, will no one save my airship?"

"Yes, I will," cried Nurse Jane, and taking her sewing thimble she ran down to the lake, dipped up water in it, and threw thimbleful after thimbleful on the blazing airship.

"Ha! That will never do!" cried the elephant. "It will take forty-seven thousand, eight hundred and ninety-two and a half thimbles full of water to put out that fire. But I can do it easily. Watch!"

With that he sucked up nearly the whole lake of water in his trunk, and then, with one puff, like that of a fireman's hose, the elephant squirted the water on the burning Chinese lanterns of the airship.

"Hiss!" went the fire, like a snake, and then it went

The elephant squirted water on the burning airship.

out, and only the lanterns were burned—not the airship at all.

"Oh, that was awfully good of you!" cried Uncle Wiggily, clapping his paws at the elephant. "I guess I had better not try to use any lighted lanterns on my airship." And he did not, at least not then.

So this shows you it is a good thing, sometimes, to have an elephant with you to squeeze out lemons, and on the next page, if the rose on our rubber plant doesn't turn into a pansy and make a pretty face at the rag doll, I'll tell you about Uncle Wiggily and the cricket.

Uncle Wiggily and the Cricket

"WHY, UNCLE Wiggily, whatever is the matter?" asked Nurse Jane Fuzzy Wuzzy, the muskrat lady, one afternoon, as she saw the rabbit gentleman sitting sad and lonely, all by himself, on a bench in the back yard, of the new hollow-stump bungalow he had built in the country. He was looking at a place where a sunflower had died because it did not get water enough to drink.

"Oh, there is nothing the matter," Uncle Wiggily said, in a doleful tone. A doleful tone is when the church organ plays away down deep in its throat, rumbly-like, and sad. "There is nothing the matter," said the bunny uncle.

"Oh, yes there is!" insisted Nurse Jane. "You would not sit out here all by yourself, looking at nothing at all, and never smiling, unless something were the matter. I am sure something must have happened. Have you the toothache, or does your rheumatism hurt you worse than usual?"

"Well, to tell you the truth, since you have asked me," spoke Uncle Wiggily, "I have the blues."

"Oh, my goodness me! The blues!" cried Nurse Jane. "You don't look blue. But you had better see Dr. Possum at once. Are the blues catching?"

"No, not exactly," answered Uncle Wiggily. "The blues are not like that. They are inside you. It is just when you feel sad, and think that everything is going wrong, and that you have no friends, no home—nothing at all to

62

make you happy—that is the blues, and I have them dreadful bad!"

"Wouldn't it do any good to have Dr. Possum?" asked Nurse Jane.

"Well, he could not give me any medicine to cure the blues," spoke Uncle Wiggily. "Though he might talk to me, and cheer me up. Sometimes doctors can do that."

"But what makes you blue?" asked Nurse Jane. "Nothing has happened, has there? You have a home, you had a nice time camping on Candy Island in Sugar Lake, and I am positive I am a good friend of yours. You have everything to be thankful for, I'm sure."

"And that's just it!" exclaimed Uncle Wiggily. "Nothing has happened, and, really, I ought to be very happy. But I am not. I guess I don't know what is the matter, except that I am cross and unhappy, and have the blues. And you had better run away, Nurse Jane, before I get the blues so bad that I tickle you with my crutch. Sometimes when rabbits have the blues they do things they are sorry for afterward."

"Oh, dear! This is too bad!" cried Nurse Jane. "I think I shall have to telephone for Dr. Possum," she said to herself, as she went in the hollow-stump house, holding her tail up out of the dust.

But before Nurse Jane had a chance to telephone for Dr. Possum, something happened. The muskrat lady was just about to call up the animal physician, when she heard a knock at the door. Going to open it she saw a cricket gentleman standing on the mat. And, on the doormat, in large letters was the word:

WELCOME

"Ha!" exclaimed the cricket gentleman, with a jolly smile, as he read the word "welcome" and made a bow. "I see you are glad to see me. Well, I will not keep you

She saw a cricket gentleman standing on the mat.

long," he chirped to Nurse Jane. "All I wish is a cup of carrot coffee, and a slice of turnip bread. Then I will be on my way," and he whistled a jolly tune, and flapped his patched and worn coat tails backward and forward.

Then Nurse Jane noticed that the cricket gentleman had on very ragged clothes, and broken shoes, and that he was very poor-looking indeed.

"Oh, I am so sorry for you!" she cried.

"Why?" asked the cricket, scratching his ear with his front leg.

"Because you are hungry, you have no nice clothes, you have no place to stay and eat, else you would not be begging from door to door. I am sorry for you," said Nurse Jane.

"You need not be sorry!" chirped the cricket. "I am as happy as can be. I can smell the beautiful flowers, I can watch the roses bloom, and hear the birds sing, and the brooks tinkle as they flow over the mossy stones. I have ragged clothes, it is true, but they are much cooler than those without holes. I am hungry, now and again, but I find friends to feed me, so I do not have to cook. In short, I am happy."

"Happy!" cried Nurse Jane. "Say no more. You are the very one I want to see. Listen, as the telephone girl says. Uncle Wiggily has the blues very bad. I don't know what they are, but he has them."

"I know what they are!" said the cricket whistling a dance tune.

"Well, perhaps then, you can cure him," said Nurse Jane. "He has everything to make him happy, but he is sad."

"I'll see what I can do," promised the cricket. So after he had eaten a grass and carrot sandwich, he hopped out to where Uncle Wiggily sat alone, still sad and disconsolate. And not letting himself be seen, the cricket sang his song:

"I was quite cold and hungry,
    My clothes were full of holes.
I had no place to eat or sleep,
    My shoes were without soles.

But now I am quite happy,
    My joy I'll never lose,
The reason is, because, you see,
    I never have the blues."

"What's that!" cried Uncle Wiggily, jumping up. "You never have the blues? How do you manage it?"

"Why every time I feel sad," said the cheerful cricket, hopping into view, "I think of some one who is worse off than I am—say an angleworm, for instance, who cannot chirp or jump. Then I am happy once more, and I go on my way most jolly-like."

"Say, that is good advice," said Uncle Wiggily, whose blue color was slowly fading away. "Let me see, of whom can I think who is worse off than I am?"

"A gold fish," said the cricket quickly. "A gold fish!"

"Why?" asked Uncle Wiggily, as if it were a riddle.

"Because, if a gold fish comes out of the water he will die," said the cricket. "You are much better off than a gold fish, even if he is beautiful, for you can live out of the water, and he cannot."

"To be sure I am!" cried Uncle Wiggily. "I never thought of that! I feel better already. Come, we will go down the street and buy ice cream cones for all the animal children we meet."

And they did. The cricket chirped, and played the fiddle with his left hind leg, and Uncle Wiggily was so happy thinking of the gold fish, and of the ice cream cones he was going to buy, that the blues no longer bothered him.

"Ha! I am very happy now!" cried the rabbit gentleman, as he bought forty-'leven ice cream cones for all his animal children friends. "You have made me very happy, Mr. Cricket."

"Then I am happy too," said the cricket, as he whistled a jolly tune. Which shows you that if you ever get the blues, and feel cross or sad, the best way to get rid of them is to try and make some one happy.

So we have come to the end of this book, for you can see for yourself there isn't room for another story in it. And if I write any more about the rabbit gentleman I shall have to put the stories in another book. So I'll say goodbye until that book comes out.